HAPPEN STANCE

MATILDA MARTEL

For my husband,
who always believed we were soul mates.
And for anyone who found love by pure happenstance.

Chapter 1
Lawson

Let's get one thing straight--- I'm not a mob lawyer. The mere insinuation that I'm in league with organized crime makes my hackles rise, and my blood pressure hits the ceiling. I run a legitimate practice and have always been selective about the clients I represent. As much as I hate to stand in judgment against fellow members of the bar, I consider those attorneys a stain on my profession.

So why did I catch a last-minute flight to meet Enzo Lupo, don of the Lupo family, in Vegas? I can answer that in one word: friendship.

I'm not his lawyer. If the state of New York brought him up on the well-deserved charge of racketeering, no amount of money could persuade me to represent him. But Enzo and I practically grew up together. We've known each other since our first year in college, and although I'm typically a horrible friend, he's always had my back. He asked me to witness his wedding and ensure his last will and testament were in order. He's a dangerous man who lives a dangerous life, but he cares for the people he loves.

As far as I can tell, he loves his bride and wants to make

sure she's taken care of if any worse-case scenarios should arise. I respect that. He may be a hardened criminal, but he's a man of his word. If he needs my help with something as simple as paperwork, I see no reason not to offer my services to an old friend.

"Mr. Kent?" A tall man in a three-piece suit approaches me at the bottom of the escalator. "Lawson Kent?"

I nod and hesitate before handing him my bag. "And you are?" You can't be too careful. Enzo has enemies, and ever since he stole his bride from the lunatic Lombardo family, those enemies have grown exponentially. I have a feeling that's why I'm here. His consigliere recently married into the Lombardos, and his loyalties may be under suspicion.

"I'm Vince---Vincent Caruso. I work for Mr. Lupo. May I take your bags?" He wrenches them out of my grip and pivots towards the sliding doors. I hate this world. I'm an officer of the court and have no business dealing with members of the underworld. If it was anyone else but Enzo, I'd be on the next plane to New York before we reached the car.

"Where is Enzo?" I unbutton my coat and throw it over my arm. I can't stop sweating, and I doubt there will be much time to change before the ceremony.

Vincent stands in front of the car door and signals me to get in. "Enzo is at the penthouse. The ceremony starts in two hours, and he's eager to get things settled before they walk down the aisle. He apologizes he couldn't meet you himself, but we're in a heightened state of security." I climb into the backseat and wait for him to circle the car. When he takes the driver's seat, he continues, "Gio Lombardo wants his daughter back. Divo Talerico wants his bride.

Neither are used to hearing no, but both are too spooked to start a war with the Lupos."

I lean into the leather seat and consider my options. What the hell have I gotten myself into? I should leave---I hate Vegas. There's nothing here but tourists, gamblers, and mobsters.

And how the hell did Enzo marry before me? It's not even an arranged marriage. The little shit fell head over heels in love, kidnapped another man's bride, and by some miracle, he won her heart. *Figures*. Enzo Lupo must have been born under a lucky star.

Not me. The one time I thought I'd fallen in love, I fell out of it just as fast. She was a great girl, and we carried on our sham love affair for almost a year. We were too busy to notice how unhappy we were. But the closer we got to the altar, the more we realized we couldn't keep fooling ourselves. Maggie had the good sense to call off the wedding, and to this day, I thank her for it.

But that doesn't mean I've given up. She's out there. For all I know, she's somewhere in this godforsaken city.

I've had a strange feeling all day. Call it intuition, or maybe it's just a hunch, but there's a reason I boarded that plane. My head told me to decline Enzo's request. But my gut made me pack my bags and drive like a madman to LaGuardia Airport. It could be for nothing, but the ache in my heart assures me something's coming---something big and beautiful that knocks me on my ass and makes me believe in love again.

"We're here." Vincent flies out of the car and sprints to open my door. I step out and survey the landscape for any rogue assassins that might recognize me as Enzo's friend. When the coast is clear, I take my bag and head into the Sonata Hotel, Lupo's secret investment property.

"Here goes," I whisper the words and chuckle under my breath.

Please be here, darling. I'm tired of waiting for you.

* * *

"You're angry---I can feel it. Don't try to deny it. You're not half as good an actor as you believe." Enzo adjusts his tie and stares at me through the mirror, smirking as he speaks.

I continue scribbling, reading over the stack of papers he unceremoniously shoved into my hands the minute I waltzed through the door. "Why would I be angry?" I tense under his gaze, then pause to read a passage on his will. "Are you sure you want to leave her so much so soon? Don't you watch true-crime documentaries? The wife always knocks off her husband to chase a financial windfall. Well, either that or another man."

He stiffens then gives me a deadly glance. He lifts his index finger and snaps, "Number one---why would I watch true crime? My life is one crime after another. I don't need to sit in front of a television and feast on the misery of others sensationalized for entertainment purposes."

I open my mouth to interrupt him, but he holds up a second finger and cuts me off. "Number two---not my Gala. You wouldn't understand because you've never truly been in love." Enzo smooths the lapels of his hand-tailored tuxedo while he speaks, "Have you ever seen me like this? I thought love would make me weak, but it's done the complete opposite. I feel more powerful than ever. My heart is full, my life has purpose, and my girl is nothing less than an angel sent from heaven to redeem me." He ends with a heavy sigh and snaps his fingers. "Which is why I need you to make sure those papers are airtight."

I slide the stack into an envelope and hand it over. "Everything looks good. What exactly are you afraid of?" My gaze shifts from him to the four bodyguards standing by. Enzo's men are always prepared for a fight, but these guys look like they're ready to go to war.

He points to my briefcase. "Keep them safe. I trust you more than I do anyone else in my organization. Nothing is more important than securing Gala's future. I'm not going anywhere any time soon. I've got a new lease on life, and I want to be around to love my wife for as long as I can. But if God has other plans, my girl will know I took care of her and our baby." He winks and stifles a grin, thrilled to be saying that last part out loud.

"Baby, huh?" I stuff the envelope in my case and stand to leave. "I'm certain you once assured me you weren't the marrying type and then double-downed insisting you'd never bring children into your twisted world."

"Love makes you do crazy things, my friend." He checks his watch, tightens a cufflink, and heads out to search for his teenage bride. "Get dressed. I marry the love of my life in thirty minutes, and no one keeps her waiting."

I watch Enzo disappear into the hall and mumble words of bitter regret. That makes three friends marrying within weeks of one another after falling ass-first into love. All this talk of soul mates, true love, and babies makes me feel like the only girl without a date to the prom.

This isn't the time to moan and complain about the state of my life. I feel ridiculous and self-centered. Today isn't about me. As his friend, I should celebrate his happiness, not agonize about my own shortcomings. He may have shunned love in the past, but I know him well enough to understand he never truly gave up hope of finding the perfect girl. And now he has.

Lucky little shit.

Who kidnaps a woman the night before her wedding to another man and still manages to make her fall madly in love with him? Enzo--- that's who. He never fails to come out on top no matter how low he sinks. Despite his never-ending good fortune, I'm still happy for him.

Not overjoyed---*just happy*.

Chapter 2
Willow
Earlier that day

UNBELIEVABLE. I STAB FURIOUSLY INTO MY PHONE'S screen and mumble curse words under my breath. I don't deserve this. Nobody deserves the aggravation of working with Baron Caulfield, Hollywood's latest bad boy extraordinaire. Ambition made me take him on as a client, but the return on my time investment has yet to pay off.

This is the last time I'm getting him out of a jam. After the weekend, I'm giving Baron his walking papers, taking a few days off to recuperate, and returning to my regular schedule.

In my world, *regular* is relative. My life is one shit show after the next, but I know how to keep things under control. Baron's shenanigans have begun to destroy my peace, and I won't allow that to happen. It's time to cut him off before he drags me into the muck with him.

"Willow! You're here!" Sebastian Luna, Baron's long-suffering personal assistant and sometime-best friend, charges toward me with outstretched arms. The crazed grin plastered across his handsome mug doesn't quite reach his bloodshot eyes. He's no doubt as sleep-deprived as me.

"Don't Willow me." I narrow my gaze and pout with utter frustration. "Why didn't you keep him on a shorter leash? You promised me you'd tighten the reins after his last break-up. Strippers? Escorts? For heaven's sake, he's got a Disney movie coming out in four months. And now, Truman Kane is rethinking hiring him for his next project," I growl and hand him my heavier bag. "Please take this. All this tension is making my neck cramp."

He nods and releases the breath he's been holding since I started my rant. "You know he's impossible. But I swear this one isn't as bad as it seems. She wasn't an escort, just a crazy fan who threw herself at him when he was drunk. Nothing happened, I swear. The paparazzi snapped that photo seconds before he pushed her away," He sighs with regret. "I don't know what's gotten into him lately, but he refuses to confide in me anymore. We should go---everyone is waiting upstairs.

I follow Seb into the gold-tinted elevators, taking two steps at a time to keep up with his long stride. I hold my fingers to my wrist and feel my heartbeat accelerate to a gallop. By the time we scoot into the crowded box, my breath exits my lungs in short pants, and beads of sweat dot my forehead. In a few short minutes, I'll be surrounded by Baron's gang of handlers, the ones who only tell him what he wants to hear. None of them show genuine friendship or compassion for a young guy struggling with his celebrity. Baron is nothing more than a means to an end. As long as he brings in millions to line their pockets, they'll indulge his vices and smackdown anyone who sets him straight. Keeping him high or drunk 24/7 makes him easier to swindle. *It makes me sick.*

At the sound of the bell, I shoot through the sliding doors and make a beeline to the suite at the end of the hall. I can't wait to see what kind of condition he's in. Seb's right about one thing. Baron hasn't been himself lately. For the past six months, he's wallowed deep in the mother of all funks, and it is high time we stop tiptoeing around his precious, fragile ego.

"Where is he?" I storm through the double doors, toss my bag on the floor and scan the room for Baron's wild auburn hair. A man in a blue pin-striped suit approaches me with a stern expression. I've never met him before, but I can already tell we won't get along.

"He's resting. He had a long night and needs to recoup." He holds out his hands like a referee and condescends to tell me my job.

"Then I'll wake him up. I didn't fly in from New York to hear him snore. We have work to do before his press junket tomorrow, and I want him to turn in early tonight." I ignore his warnings and push past Seth, Baron's beefy bodyguard, too tired to put up a fight and holding on by a thread. Like his brother Sebastian, he looks like he hasn't slept in days.

"Dear Lord!" I burst into the pitch-black bedroom to find Baron Caulfield's very round and incredibly firm ass emerging through a set of tangled sheets. A lone ray of sunshine peeks through the heavy curtains and illuminates nothing but his untanned cheeks. Why would someone sleep naked in the middle of the day?

"Sorry, Willow." Seth scrambles towards the bed and throws a crumpled comforter over the offending sight. He offers a shy smile then shakes his head with disapproval. "Please, talk some sense into him before he burns out. He won't admit it to me, but I'm pretty sure he's in love."

Stunned by this revelation, I trip over my feet. "In love? Baron doesn't love anyone but himself." I pull the curtains back and let the Vegas sun flood the room. Baron squeals in agony and shoves his head under the pillow. His flawless body twists and curls into the fetal position, groaning for relief from the harsh sounds of mine and Seth's whispering voices.

I wish I could sympathize. As much as I complain about his reckless and cavalier attitude towards his career, no one suffers more than him. He's lived most of his life under the spotlight and has every wrong decision dissected under a microscope.

Fame is not for the faint of heart.

"Up and at 'em, big boy." I snatch the pillow out of his hands and swat him once in the back of the head. "I know you feel like shit, but you asked for my help, and I came. I don't care how many awards you've won. You're not taking a nap on my time."

"Willow, please," Baron whines and digs under the covers like my grandmother's dachshund. "My head is killing me. I can't do those junkets. I just can't."

He peers up from under the covers, clutching his pillow tightly to his chest. "How do I get out of this? I want to go home. I need to get back to New York. Tell them whatever you think they need to hear, and let me go home." His melancholy voice breaks my heart, but his self-sabotage grates my nerves.

I shake my head, peel off my coat and pull up the closest chair. "New York?" I stare, confused at Seth, who nods once. His sympathetic expression assures me there is more to the story. Baron hates New York. He hasn't lived there in years. As much I want to pry for more information, I've got a job to do.

"Sorry, Baron. I want to go back to New York, too. You made a commitment, and the studio paid you a ton of money to help promote the movie. No one expects you to dazzle the press. You just have to do your job, and I promise I'll have your cranky butt on a plane back to New York tomorrow night." I lean in, and my stomach sours with the smell of stale whiskey.

"Fine. I'll do one day, and then I want to leave." He flings the heavy blanket over his head and sulks. "Just give me twenty more minutes of sleep."

"No can do." I kick the box spring and ask Seth for his invaluable assistance. "Please get his whiskey-soaked ass into the shower. We've got work to do."

Chapter 3
Willow

ONCE UPON A TIME, I WANTED TO BE A TEACHER. AND not just any teacher. I wanted to teach kindergarten like my grandmother---the number one schoolteacher in Westchester County.

Nana isn't just a hell of an educator. She's the quintessential caregiver. After she teaches a room full of rambunctious five-year-olds their ABCs, she wipes noses, straightens backpacks, ties shoelaces, and watches them board the bus home. She treats her job like a mission and deserves every accolade she receives. At sixty-two, she's still going strong and dreading every year she inches closer to retirement.

That dedication comes from a genuine love for her work, and I admire the hell out of it. I wish I'd had the resolve to ignore the call of money and follow my dreams. But things turned out different for me.

Not worse, just different.

Grandpa gave her the luxury to pursue her dreams. They fell in love young, and his job in the city afforded them a comfortable life. Teachers never make a living wage-

--at least not in Manhattan. As much as I want to follow in her footsteps, I can't rely on anyone but myself. The city isn't cheap, and when you grow up with friends like mine, both daughters of billionaires, you become restless to become one of the haves and not linger with the have-nots. And that takes money---lots of it.

This job isn't so bad. Maybe I don't get enough sleep. Perhaps there's never been any time to cultivate healthy relationships with the opposite sex. But there's time for that later---or never. Who cares? Love is nothing more than a transitional emotion that comes and goes like the seasons. If my two best friends weren't hopelessly in love and on the verge of diving deep into the ocean of matrimony, I would never give this a second thought.

I mean, who the hell becomes engaged in a matter of weeks? That's ludicrous and dangerously optimistic.

I really need to stop internalizing this shit. Jana and Macy are my two best friends in the whole wide world, and I swear I'm happy for them. Not delighted---just happy.

Don't get me wrong. I'm thrilled they're blissfully in love, and I hope they beat the odds. But my crushing loneliness makes me a selfish jerk who can't stop replaying my own inadequacies in my twisted, anxiety-ridden brain.

It'll pass. By the time I walk down that aisle dressed in whatever horrid outfit they make me wear, I promise I'll be smiling from ear to ear. And then I'll dance the night away with whatever hapless fool I can convince to attend.

Dear Lord, what on earth happened to me?

I used to be a cheerleader---all bubbles and flip flops. This job and the pampered poodles I deal with day in and day out have left me jaded and in search of a smoking habit. No, I can't do that. Cigarettes wreak havoc on your skin, and I plan on being a frisky old lady chasing younger men until my eighties.

"Willow, let me walk you to your room. Rumor has it there's a mob wedding happening somewhere in this hotel. It's not safe." Seth grabs my bags and leads me into the hall.

"Mob? Are you serious?" I look from side to side, expecting to find swarthy men lurking behind potted plants and peering through peepholes. "What are they doing here?"

He chuckles to himself as we head towards the elevators. "Enzo Lupo owns this hotel. Didn't you know?"

My brain trips and stumbles in my skull, dazed by his words. "Lupo? Are you kidding me? Why are we staying in a mob-owned hotel? There are tons of nice hotels on the strip. Don't we have enough problems with Baron's image?" I pick up my lazy pace and slip through the sliding steel doors. Seth is hot on my heels.

He shakes his head and taps the button to the fiftieth floor. I prefer keeping my distance from Baron's entourage in case things grow loud or out of hand. "Baron loves this hotel. He insisted. And when he insists, we just go with the flow. Besides, the Sonata has no equal. They might be criminals, but those mobsters spare no expense when it comes to customer service." He holds the doors open and watches me stagger out onto the plush burgundy carpet, unable to contradict his opinion. This place is a freaking palace.

"Do you think I'll be safe in the hotel lounge? I need a drink, and I don't want to inhale an entire bottle of wine alone in my room. It feels wrong and unhinged." I slide my keycard into the reader and take my bags from his steely grip.

He purses his lips and attempts to speak, stopping himself as he changes course. "Do you want me to send down Sebastian? I'd go with you, but I need to make sure Baron doesn't try to sneak out in the middle of the night." He squints with annoyance, probably regretting his career choice as much as me.

"No, I'll be fine. I heard jazz humming through the lobby, the kind of music my grandparents listened to when I was younger. All I want to do is unwind with a stiff martini and listen to that Frank Sinatra impersonator belt out my Nana's favorite songs. No conversation. No hook-ups. Just me and my drink, silent as the grave." I give him a wink and sneak into my room, grateful for the peace, quiet, and unspeakable luxury of the corner suite. Baron might be a pain in the ass, but he knows how to make it up to people.

"Text me when you get back in your room---okay?" Seth commands as he makes his exit. "No excuses, Willow. I hear Enzo is the one getting married. If that's true, then this place is crawling with gangsters."

"The don?" I sneak back into my room and bolt the door. Maybe I'll order in.

Chapter 4
Lawson

DOES ANYONE REALLY ENJOY WEDDINGS? IT'S SAFE TO assume the wedding couple has their fair share of fun. At least, they should. What's the purpose of dishing out that kind of dough if you don't relish every moment of sealing your life to the person of your dreams?

Gala and Enzo hardly noticed anyone else in the room. That's the way it should be. Their guests are nothing more than props to wish them well---a captive audience to bear witness to their magical love. The night was heavy with inappropriate displays of affection, and the air was thick with communal bitterness. Or was it just me?

Anyway, I'm glad I made my escape. It's terrible luck to wallow in self-pity in the presence of true love. And although it's a little too fast and furious for my taste, there's no doubt they're madly in love. Enzo is now a happily married man, and I'm still the carefree bachelor I've always been.

Why concern myself with changing what works?

One hour of pretending to socialize with people who either frighten me or ask for free legal advice is about all I can take. If Enzo was looking at anyone but his bride, I would have given him my farewell, but he won't notice me gone. He and Gala are floating on cloud nine and dancing on top of the world. I'm pleased he's found someone to share his life with. It's not easy being him. He inherited his position from his old man and has taken great pains to make the best of a life he never wanted. If this young lass brings him joy, then I lift my glass of whiskey and wish them well.

Now, all I need is that glass.

I tap the M button on the keypad and head to the Mezzanine. Enzo's lounge boasts the best Frank Sinatra impersonator on both coasts. He imported him directly from New Jersey and loves him so much he gives him free room and board here at the hotel. I heard him belting out a few tunes on my way in. I just hope he hasn't gone on an extended break or fled to join the wedding. Frank Sinatra is just the kind of pick-me-up I could use right about now.

My parents loved his music and played that kind of stuff around the house throughout my childhood. I'm not that old---they are. I'm the youngest of three brothers and the surprise baby thirteen years into my parents' marriage.

Shocking, I know. That is what they get for acting like teenagers. My brothers are almost a decade older than me, and there were no plans to continue the Kent brood when the doctor came calling with news that the rabbit died---so to speak. Poor Mama was beside herself. A good southern woman and a pillar of Clemson, South Carolina society didn't expect to find herself knocked up at the age of thirty-nine, but she hoped for the best and prayed I'd be the baby girl who eluded her in her younger years.

She was wrong. I was bigger and beefier than my brothers. But being the baby, I soon became her favorite.

And I know she worries about me. I'm thirty-five years

old, and I'm no closer to giving her grandchildren than I was in high school. Fortunately, my brothers have come through in that department and bought me enough time to do things right. But Mama still insists she'd like to be young enough to chase them around her garden.

"Just follow your heart, Law." Those are her sage words whenever I say I'm not in the mood for another failed relationship. And I keep repeating them in my head as I follow the music into the dimly lit lounge at the end of the hall. As I step through the beaded drape, I spot a lovely woman sitting at the grand piano belting out her version of Satin Doll. The lounge is nearly empty, except for a few night owls. I lift my wrist to check the time and realize it's almost midnight. Fake Frank must have headed upstairs to grab some cake.

I can't blame him. It might be the best cake I've ever had.

"Would you like a table, sir?" A gentleman greets me with a menu, but I wave him off. "I'll sit at the bar if that's okay."

He nods and points in the direction of the bartender, busy at work mixing a martini and flirting with a flaxen-haired knockout sitting alone. The poor girl chose to come here alone, and he's taken it upon himself to entertain her because she's beautiful. If she was a pinch less attractive, he wouldn't bother. Nevertheless, he considers himself a hero for stepping up and keeping her company.

I amble closer and catch the bored expression on her gorgeous face. My heart flutters wildly, but I temper my enthusiasm and pace. Why wouldn't I be excited to see a woman as stunning as her? It means nothing. I see beautiful women every day. Maybe none affect me like this, but I'm tired, and I've just spent the last hour watching two people proclaim their undying love for one another. I'm obviously in a vulnerable state.

"What can I get you?" The hipster bartender stops sexually harassing the blonde doll long enough to do his job.

I climb onto a barstool a few seats away from the angel and try to peel my eyes from her long enough not to slide off the polished leather. My breath comes in pants, and my heartbeat accelerates. I watch her lashes flutter, and my skin prickles with premonition.

Fate led me here. I know it like I know my name.

Her pouty lips grip the edge of her martini glass, and filthy thoughts invade my wistful mind. What's happening to me? Beneath the bar, strange things evolve of their own accord, and with little provocation, my cock hardens and tests the fabric of my trousers. She faces forward, disinterested in the perverted man lurking nearby. Good for her. Set your standards higher than this old geezer, sweetheart. No doubt she's a model or aspiring actress---but maybe not. I've never seen her before, and God knows I'd remember a face like hers.

"Can I get a whiskey neat, please? Thank you." I grumble then pull out my wallet, handing him my credit card to start a tab. I should sneak away to a table and leave this poor woman to her thoughts, but I can't force myself to retreat to the shadows. Even if we don't speak a word to one another, my night feels better for having lived in her orbit for just a few minutes.

"Are you here for a convention?" My eyes grow wide at the sound of the sweetest voice I've ever heard. Chest pains ensue as my pulse climbs to an unmanageable pace. Is she talking to me? She couldn't be. I'm not Enzo. Shit like this never happens to me.

Despite what some people believe, flirting doesn't come naturally to all southerners. I'm not without my charms, but I've never been the coolest cat in the room. The only time I shine is inside a courtroom.

Men are easy to handle. Most are idiots- long-winded, grandiose, and in love with their own reflection, much like Narcissus. I can tear through them one by one, gain the upper hand and never break a sweat. But women are different. To me, they're the personification of love because they're the best mankind has to offer.

They are soft and hard, curvy in all the right places, naughty at all the right times, and far more intelligent than men. My Daddy taught me to never believe you know more than them---especially about those sweet little details that make them tick. Stand back, son and let your woman shine---you won't be sorry.

Unfortunately, he didn't teach me much about wooing a woman. At the age of fifteen, he met my mother and settled his heart on her and her alone. They just celebrated their fifty-fifth wedding anniversary, and I swear on a stack of bibles, they still shower together. That's quite an example and one I hope I can follow.

I tilt my head to face the beauty to my right, channeling Enzo's debonair moves and confident I won't do them justice. Bright blue eyes, the color of the sky after a summer rain, meet mine, and my heart melts into an unrecognizable lump in my stomach. It'll never be whole again until I make her mine.

I found her. My girl is here in this miserable, godforsaken city, and she made the first move---because God knows I'd never feel worthy enough to be so bold.

But now she's opened the door and *help me, Jesus*, I'm barging all the way in.

Chapter 5
Willow

WHAT IN THE WORLD AM I DOING? I NEVER TALK TO strange men in bars. I came here for peace and quiet, and I've spent the last half hour bombarded with one cheap line after another from a bartender who spends far too much time on his perfect hair. Why do men think we care about their beauty regimen? I don't even want to discuss my own. It's boring and self-indulgent.

But this big guy seems different. He ordered a whiskey neat---I like that. My grandpa drinks whiskey neat. It's a real man's drink---down to earth, old-fashioned, and no-frills. That's the vibe I get from him. I don't know who he is or where he came from, but his rugged masculine features are a feast for my lonely, sex-starved eyes.

"No, I'm here on business and to attend the wedding of a dear friend." His deep southern drawl hits me like a hormonal tidal wave and stuns me into temporary silence. My tummy roils with unexpected jitters, and my heart skips a beat---maybe two.

"Wedding?" I stammer like a schoolgirl who's finally worked up the nerve to speak to her longtime crush, and I grip the smooth mahogany wood in front of me for purchase. "The Lupo wed..." I cut my words when I realize I'm prying into his business. He doesn't seem like the kind of man who would fraternize with gangsters, but perhaps I'm mistaken. It's his accent. He's obviously from the south. How would he know Enzo Lupo?

He offers an almost imperceptible nod and lifts the glass of whiskey to his lips. My hungry gaze follows the path, awestruck by his sinewy hand and thick beefy fingers. I lick my lips and slowly cross my legs, unconsciously rubbing my thighs together.

The handsome man points to the barstool next to mine and whispers, "May I?"

I swallow the saliva pooling in my mouth and chirp something that sounds like a yes. Warmth blooms on my cheeks as I shimmy back into my seat, trying my best to suck in my non-existent gut now that he's less than a foot away.

Holy crap, he smells delicious.

This is disgraceful. I should leave now before I hand this strange man my panties and tell him to make me his bad girl. But goddamn, I want to be his bad girl. And deep down, maybe his good girl too.

"Does everyone in the hotel know about Enzo's wedding upstairs?" His dreamy drawl makes his statement seem perfectly innocent, like Enzo is just the guy who runs the local Italian trattoria and not the head of New York's five families.

I nod, then shrug, hoping to appear disinterested when I'm honestly at the edge of my seat. "I'm not sure what everyone knows. My client's bodyguard told me. He tends to be in the know about these things. If it wasn't for him, I'd probably be clueless."

A smile tugs at the full lips peeking through his heavy

beard, and my legs quiver with need, instinctively parting to offer the goods. Good Lord, when did I become such a tramp? The man hasn't even bought me a drink.

"I'm not affiliated with organized crime. Enzo and I attended law school together and kept in touch over the years. He asked me for impartial legal advice and invited me to attend. I couldn't say no. I won't make any excuses for him, but I know a different side---a kinder side than most. My name is Lawson, Lawson Kent." He extends his hand, and the name instantly strikes a chord of familiarity. "With whom do I have the pleasure?"

His old-fashioned manners make me sway in my stool. I sink my teeth into my bottom lip to stifle an inappropriate giggle and let my trembling hand slide into his oversized mitt. When he covers and caresses it gently, I nearly swoon to the floor. "I'm Willow...Willow Munro." I hear the words float between us, but I'm too dazed to feel them leave my lips.

"Willow Munro?" His brow creases, and his shoulders slack before his slight grin slithers into a gorgeous smile that takes up half his face. I could stare at that gorgeous smile all day long. "From New York? Macy's Willow?"

I lean back as the sharp pain of dread stabs my heart. Macy? Lawson? That's why his name sounds familiar. He's her lawyer friend. Oh, no---is this deliberate? She wanted me to bring him, and I specifically told her she was out of her mind. Is this an elaborate ruse to prove me wrong?

"You know Macy Ramos?" I stutter, blinking furiously, unsure of what to make of this revelation, and silently berating myself for not taking Macy up on her earlier offer. For months, I've had disastrous dates with self-absorbed pretty boys when this strapping hunk of a man was only a phone call away.

Why am I so stubborn?

He leans in, giving me a generous but cruel whiff of his panty-melting cologne, although I suspect it's nothing more than his manly scent mixed with the sweet smell of his whiskey. "Why on earth did Macy think you needed fixin' up? You're breathtaking. Right now, I want to kick myself in the nuts---pardon my language---for dismissing all her attempts."

I guffaw. No, good God, I snort. I slap my mouth to my face to muffle my hyena laugh and poke my eye with my index finger. With one eye watering profusely, I try to compose myself long enough to speak and keep him from bolting to his room. "What are the odds? Did Macy tell you I'd be here? My client has a press junket tomorrow, and she knew I didn't want to come alone. She suggested I bring you, but I hate fix-ups."

He reaches into his coat pocket and pulls out a neatly folded handkerchief. "Here you go. I promise it's fresh from the laundry."

I stare transfixed at the initials LAK embroidered into the tightly spun fabric of his cotton handkerchief and release a tiny whimper, "You carry handkerchiefs with you?"

"It's an antiquated practice, I know. But it's a habit I learned from my granddaddy. And you were right to turn Macy down. A woman like you doesn't need a blind date--- however much it might have benefited me. You should be wooed, ambushed, and chased. Then two men should battle to the death for the pleasure of your company." He gives me a wink, and the humming sensation between my thighs begins to simmer like a rattling tea kettle.

Who the hell is this man? He's far too humble. Lawson Kent sticks out like a well-formed, well-groomed mountain man in a sea of slick New York dandies. He's rough and ready and yet a man of the world. He looks like he could chop your wood, fix your car, get you out of a legal jam and then fuck your troubles away. I'll admit I'm intrigued and I can't be the first to notice.

"I could say the same about you. Why would Macy think you need to be fixed up? Surely, you've got girls eating out of your hand." I take a sip of what's left of my martini and hope that didn't sound offensive. So much of what I say comes out much harsher than I intended. I didn't grow up with siblings---or parents, for that matter. My grandparents raised me, and they're both the most direct people you'll ever meet.

He lifts his soft brown gaze to mine, and a part of my heart escapes my chest and lands safely in his meaty grip. Panic rises within, and I consider making my much overdue escape. Everything about this evening has not gone according to plan. And I'm a girl who sticks to the program.

I was supposed to enjoy a quiet evening alone listening to fake Frank Sinatra, not flirting my tits off with a man who not only has my number but he also can't stop dialing it.

"Darling, there is no comparison between you and me. You are the sun, and I am the moon. I may glow, but you light up the whole damn world." His voice never wavers. His eyes never leave mine. I'd say that's the dumbest thing I'd ever heard, but I can't. What little remains of my heart promptly flees into his grasp, and my eyes mist with unshackled bliss.

Thank goodness my eyes are already red from the earlier mishap.

He takes my hands and helps me off the stool. "Everything happens for a reason. I'm not supposed to be here. Not in Vegas. Not at this bar. For the first time in my life, I believe in fate."

"You do?" I place my hand in his, and tiny sparks of electricity flowing through us make my skin prickle.

He nods and lifts my hand to his lips. "Forgive me for being so bold. But come out with me. Let's have a bit of fun and paint this miserable town red. I want to get to know you better."

Holy shit, I think I'm in love.

Chapter 6
Lawson

A little more than a year ago, I swore off sex. Not permanently, of course, just until marriage. The timing seemed strange since I was engaged to be married, but I explained it was best if we cool things down and concentrated on the emotional side of our union. On the upside, we wouldn't have to wait long. Our wedding was less than three months away.

My then-fiancée, Maggie, wasn't happy about my decision and questioned my fidelity. If I wasn't getting it from her, was I getting it from someone else? I assured her that wasn't the case. I'm a one-woman man through and through. Three weeks later, she called off the wedding---just like I expected. Sex was the driving force between us, and once I took it away, she realized what an empty, shallow existence we shared. In hindsight, I knew from the start things were destined to end.

Sometimes you just know how things will turn out.

I don't need days, weeks, months, or years to figure out that Willow Munro is the woman meant to be my wife. I don't need to make love to her to know she's destined to be the mother of my children. The feeling is so palpable I can smell it in the air.

We're not here by happenstance---this is fate. I feel it in my bones.

Speaking of bones---I really wish I hadn't sworn off sex. I swear to Christ, I'm harder than a slab of granite. One more gorgeous pout from her luscious lips, and my cock is liable to burst free from my pants and knock this table on its side. I don't know how the hell I'll survive the rest of this evening without hitching that dress over her waist and licking my way up her thighs.

Lord, have mercy. Why must you tempt me so cruelly?

"Wait a minute---did you say you met Enzo at law school? Were you joking?" She taps the tip of her napkin to her puffy lips, and I grit my teeth, summoning the fortitude and strength of mind to find the words to answer her.

I growl, willing my cock to go down. There isn't enough blood in my brain to recall those memories, but I do my best. "Hand to God at Harvard Law." I lift my hand to buy myself a few seconds of precious time. I bring the glass of brandy to my lips and scan the recesses of my mind while her big blue doe eyes wait with the sweet anticipation of a child. My heart melts for the umpteenth time tonight, and I steady my nerves. I can't let my lady down. "Would you believe he was first in our class?"

"No?!" She slams her hand on the table, shocked by my admission. "Why would a mobster go to law school?"

I watch her eyes sparkle with a morbid curiosity I know too well and humor her for a few minutes more. "Enzo is his father's second son and should have been his older brother's consigliere---his lawyer and advisor."

She stops me. "I've seen the Godfather. You mean someone like Tom Hagen."

I chuckle and continue, "Of course, great movie. Their dad, the old don, wanted him to attend Harvard. Enzo got in on his own merit---he insisted. He may be a criminal, but he's got some weird ethical line he won't cross. I don't understand how he reconciles the two in his mind, but he does. Shortly after our freshman year, his brother went missing, and they found the poor guy chained to a pier in the East River a few days later. That made Enzo the heir apparent and..."

"No more law school..." She finishes my sentence.

"Bingo." I tip my glass in her direction and quickly change the subject. "Enough about that. I don't want to talk about other people. I want to know every little detail about Miss Willow Munro. Macy tells me you babysit celebrities and get them out of jams. Do you like your job?"

She smiles coquettishly, and my cock scrapes the back of my zipper. I yelp into my glass but keep my eyes focused on the angel sitting across from me. She's a breath of fresh air in this den of iniquity.

"Some days, it's fun. These big stars fall apart, and I'm the person who can make their problems go away. It makes me feel important---you know? Growing up, I never felt important. But when I'm at work, all eyes are on me, and people get out of my way. My clients need me." She shoots me a childish grin that almost reaches her eyes. I'm not convinced. Something is dimming those bright blue eyes, and I won't let that stand.

"Why didn't you feel important? Too many siblings?" I shamelessly pry.

She shakes her head and nibbles on an appetizer. "I'm an only child. Macy and our other friend, Jana, are the closest I've ever come to having sisters. Do you know Jana?"

I nod. "Very well. Her soon-to-be-husband takes up half

of my practice." I pause to drink her in. It's so easy to get lost in every inch of this glorious woman I'd quickly forget where I am. I need to focus, and more importantly, I need to stop letting her change the subject. She doesn't want to talk about herself. But from my end, the life and times of Willow Munro are all I want to hear.

"That's right. You work in their building." She hugs her chest and searches for some type of escape. It's a fruitless attempt. Wherever she goes, I'll be right behind her. There's no running from me, doll.

"If you were an only child, why did you feel unimportant? Why would you ever feel insignificant? You should be the center of attention wherever you go." Every word comes out like a statement for the record---like I'm arguing before the court, and my life, not my client's, depends on it.

Her soft unblinking gaze grows wide and lances my heart. A flush of crimson stains her cheeks, and her lips part with a slight tremble, "my parents are Howard and Jessica Munro."

"The news anchors?" I don't understand. Her parents are a beloved all-American institution.

She nods and rubs her biceps, suddenly cold, recalling an unsavory memory. "Work was their life. They fought hard to get where they were and couldn't take anything for granted. When they realized I was spending more time with nannies than them, they sent me to live with my grandparents in Westchester and then boarding school. We're not close. I don't see them often- some birthdays, two Christmases ago. But it worked out for the best. I love my grandparents. They more than made up for it." She shrugs like it doesn't bother her, but I know it does.

"You deserved better, darling. And you'll do better, won't you? I'll bet you'll make a great mother who'll lavish all kinds of wonderful on your babies." I lift my glass and wait for her to clink it with hers.

She freezes, surprised I've uncovered some secret desire she didn't want to share so soon. "That's sweet, but I'm not sure I'm the nurturing type."

I bring my glass all the way over and clink it into her goblet. "Forgive my presumptive nature. You've made your career out of herding adult-size brats. I assume you'd like a few miniature versions with your eyes."

A five-hundred-watt smile spreads across her lovely face and sets my world on fire. My heart explodes like a hydrogen bomb in my chest, and a plume of ash incinerates my throat. It's impossible to speak, but I need to profess words of undying love. I need to tell this wondrous girl I'll marry her this month and give her however many babies her heart desires. She'll never be lonely. She'll never feel trivial or inconsequential again. If she'll have me, I'll love her with all that I am until the day I die.

Machine-gun laughter bursts free, and she wraps her arms around her midsection, no doubt trying to settle the anxiety I've caused with my psychotic glare. "Should we get going? I think this place may be closing up." She looks past my shoulder and points to the server attempting to hand me the check.

I nod then shake my head, extending my hand to retrieve the check from the eager man waiting nearby. "This is Vegas, sweetheart. There's always something open. Let's hit a casino and have a bit of fun. You make me feel lucky."

Chapter 7
Willow

"Thirty-two, straight up." The dealer places the marker over number thirty-two and clears my stack of chips.

"Oh my God, that's me. Lawson, I won! Holy crap, I won! I won. You said thirty-two, and I played thirty-two on a whim, and I won. I won!" I jump in place, clinking my silver bangle against my watch as I clap my hands in a wild frenzy of utter delight. "What did I win? Was it a lot?"

"Yes, sweetheart. You bet a thousand on one number. You just won thirty-five thousand dollars." He wraps his arms around my waist and gives me a kiss on the cheek. The soft scruff of his beard tickles my skin, and I lean into him, wanting so much more. He hasn't laid a hand on me all night.

The dealer hands him a slip of paper, and Lawson points to me, raising a brow with critical derision. "She won, not me."

"Your winnings, ma'am. You can give this to the cashier."

"Should we keep going?" I lift my gaze to Lawson and

imagine swaying cheek to cheek under the moonlight. My God, I've got it bad.

A slight smile appears. "Let's quit while we're ahead. These guys are dying to win their money back, and it's nearly 3:00am." He offers his hand, and I walk my fingers into his palm, squeezing it as tight as I can.

"What time do you fly back to the city?" I ask while we walk, wondering if I'll see him again before we leave. We haven't made plans for tomorrow or the day after that---or the day after that. I think he likes me. He seems to like me. I'm not a good judge of this type of man. Two-dimensional men are easy to read. Lawson has all kinds of dimensions. He's real.

And I think I want real. Real feels good.

He lifts my hand to his lips and gives it a tiny peck. The touch of his kiss releases a thousand butterflies in my tummy, and I stumble in my heels. How does he make me feel sexy and naïve all at once?

"I have an early afternoon flight. I believe I leave at 1:00. What time are you done with work?" He waits nearby while I hand the cashier my credit slip. Is he asking me out? Will we go upstairs now? Why can't we go upstairs now? I'm ready. I'm willing. I'll do anything he wants---and then some.

"I'm done at 3:00, maybe 4:00. My plane leaves at 5:30, but I guess you'll be long gone by then...huh? Are you pretty tired?" I mumble through what feels like a blatant proposition. In all my years, I've never chased a man, but I've also never wanted one this much. Is that why I want him? Because he's holding out? No, I wanted him before he spoke a word.

He nods once, then smiles. "You're not getting rid of me so quickly, darling."

My heart swells and rises like a helium balloon. I tuck a few strands of hair behind my ear, having forgotten all my moves in the presence of this divine slice of man, and attempt to decipher what he means. "My suite overlooks the strip. You should come see it."

He bites his lip and squeezes my hand as he leads us towards the elevators upstairs. "Let me walk you to your room."

* * *

The doors roll open, and my feet leave the floor. "Lawson! Yes!" Our lips crash, and the weight of his hard body pins us to the back of the elevator. The air crackles with electricity as we take our first taste, and I throw my arms around his neck, crushing my breasts to his chest.

I want nothing between us—not even air.

"I've wanted to kiss you since the second I laid eyes on you," he groans and wraps one arm around the small of my back. "You don't know how hard it is to be a gentleman around you." His lips fall back on mine, but we don't kiss. We inhale the air we breathe. Lawson feasts, and I devour. We mine for each other's souls. In the span of fifty-five floors, we dry hump like teenagers against the steel wall, too horny or oblivious to care about possible interruptions. And thankfully, no one barges into our public display of desperation. Every second feels like minutes, but I want it to go on forever. With every stab of his jutting length, I imagine him thrusting brutally into my wet hot core. I want him rough, gentle, one after the other. I don't even care how I get it. If he's giving, I'm taking.

I break away, panting, but he recaptures my lips, and our mouths meld in a blistering kiss that feeds my empty heart with promises I've never heard before. Promises I want to believe. Love doesn't come easy for me. But I can show him the only brand of love I've ever known. If he'll let me.

When his giant hand slips a few inches lower and gently kneads my ass, I whimper my approval. Nothing can stop this momentum. How can anything keep me from waking up wrapped in his massive arms?

"Baby..." His raspy groan breaks our kiss and interrupts my blissful thoughts of morning pancakes. I whine as I pull away, still kissing the air.

"I'm walking you to your room, but I'm not checking out any of your lovely views---not yet. You better believe I will. But not yet," he exhales a torturous breath, and my heart sinks with loss. What? What's happening?

"Not yet?" The doors fly open, and in an act of desperate lust, I latch onto his lapels and drag him into the hallway. I'm a woman possessed. This hunger needs to be sated, and only Lawson Kent can quench this fire. Propriety be damned. "Please, Lawson, I'm so wet. And if you get any harder, you'll rip a hole in your slacks. I don't give a damn about what happens tomorrow..."

His brow creases, and his expression hardens into a scowl. He takes my hand and threads our fingers tightly as he walks me towards my door. When we reach the end of the hall, he spins me around and catches my chin. His soft brown gaze bores into me as his chest heaves, rising and falling with each labored breath. "Tomorrow is Friday, and you'll probably get home late. I want to take you to dinner on Saturday night. Are you free?"

"Dinner? Like a real date?" The butterflies fluttering in my nether regions shoot straight into my heart.

He nods and holds out his hand. "May I have your phone, please?"

I tuck my hand into my purse and snatch my cell phone, typing my password while I pass it to him. He examines it briefly then calls himself. "Now we have each other's phone numbers. I'll text you when I get to my room, and you can program my name. We have firm plans for Saturday, Willow Munro. You not caring about what happens tomorrow is precisely why we need to get to know one another better. *Because I do care.* I care about what happens tomorrow and the next day and the day after that."

I step closer, regretting my horny words and wishing I could take them back. "I'm sorry. I didn't mean what I said. It's just..."

"You can make it up to me in other ways, doll..." Lawson's gorgeous smile reappears, and I fly into his arms. His lips settle on mine, caressing my mouth with a kiss that makes me float into the clouds and brings me the sweetest dreams I've had since I was that little girl who dreamt of white knights in faraway lands.

I have a feeling this will turn out so much better.

Chapter 8
Lawson

"It's a good thing. Jumping into intimacy too soon will only give us a false sense of stability before we've built a firm foundation. And Willow and I need to stand on solid ground before we start our family. I can tell from our conversations her childhood trauma makes her question her worthiness to be loved, and that breaks my goddamn heart.

Our parents made us believe in love, and I'd like the same for mine and Willow's children. Rushing into bed might destroy everything. I can't ruin this, Lincoln. I won't!" I slam my clenched fist into my palm and stare at my older brother's face on the tiny screen across the room. He wipes the sleep from his eyes and yawns, clearly unhappy with this late-night call for brotherly advice.

"For fuck's sake, Lawson. It's 5:30 in New York. I have an appointment at 7:45, and now there's no sense in going back to bed. You said this was an emergency, not a predawn pep-talk." He walks with the phone in front of his face and mumbles profanities.

My grumpy middle brother, Lincoln, is the reason I became a lawyer then left South Carolina for New York.

I've secretly idolized him all my life, and despite his modest demeanor, he always supplies the most invaluable advice. It's worth putting up with his crankiness to squeeze a few droplets of wisdom from his old ass.

"I'll make it up to you. You know I will." I assure him of my sincerity while I watch him brush his teeth.

He gargles, twisting his features as he considers my dilemma, then wipes his mouth. "You haven't been with anyone since Maggie?"

I shake my head. "No. You know I haven't. And we stopped relations before our break-up. That was a serious point of contention on her behalf. Sex ruins things. It did for us."

His gaze narrows into tiny slits. He dabs his salt, and pepper beard with a hand towel then returns to his bedroom. "Sex ruins nothing. It's the greatest fucking thing known to man. Take it from someone who hasn't known the sweet touch of a woman's body in years." He snaps, shaking his head as he stomps through the hall.

"Your feelings ruined sex, little brother. Or shall I say your lack of feelings? Did you feel this way about Maggie on your first date?" He places his phone on his dresser and speaks to me from across his room. In a hostile act of retaliation, he disrobes and gives me a perfect shot of his naked ass heading into the closet. Fucking Lincoln.

"I never felt this much for Maggie. I'd marry Willow today without fear of consequences. I know she's the one." I answer the question and fall back onto the couch, confident that I've fallen in love for the first and last time.

"Then confess how you feel and tell her about your stupid little oath. Don't leave her hanging. Now leave me alone. I don't need to hear this so early in the morning. A woman throwing herself at you is not a problem. Five years without sex is a problem." He walks towards the phone with a towel wrapped around his waist and ends the call.

In typical fashion, he makes a good point. This is no time to play coy. For over a year, I've made myself believe I wasn't one of the fortunate ones. I'd never be one of the lucky stiffs who finds his other half. But I am, and I have. Everything happens for a reason, and Enzo's tiresome request proves it.

I didn't want to come, but I did. I flew clear across the country to meet a woman who lives five blocks from me. We booked the same hotel and walked into the same bar looking for fake Frank Sinatra. This is fate. How can I leave this city without her? At the very least, I need to tell her how I feel.

Tomorrow night isn't just our first real date---it's the first day of the rest of our lives. And I need to pull out all the stops.

With blinding clarity, I scramble across the couch and scroll through my phone. I'll have Enzo track down her information and get a seat on her flight. Is that an invasion of privacy? It doesn't matter. She said she felt invisible and neglected. Well, those days are long gone. I'm going to be all over your sweet ass night and day, my love.

But first, we'll do things right. Sex is the never-ending dessert we enjoy at the close of our get-to-know-you meal. Lincoln isn't wrong. It is the greatest thing known to man, and I'm confident enough in my sexual prowess to believe I could knock her socks off in that department.

It isn't cockiness. I work damn hard, and I'd go far beyond the call of duty to please my Willow. That girl gets my juices flowing with nothing more than a sly smile. I can't imagine what I'll feel holding her ripe naked curves in my grateful arms. The thought alone makes my head spin and my balls ache for release.

I need to make plans, call Enzo, the airlines, the florist, and make reservations for tomorrow night. Perhaps if I appeal to her emotions over her libido, she'll agree we need to take it slow. She's a sensible girl underneath that sexy exterior, and I know we'll come to a practical decision about our future. Yes, yes, slow is good. Slow is best. There's no need to unleash the beast so soon. Once he's out of his cage, there's no way I'll stuff him back in.

Delirious and sleep-deprived, I mumble to myself as I check the airline app on my phone. I tap through a long line of urgent messages and try to read through each one. *All NYC flights canceled due to inclement weather. Call your agent to reschedule.*

Well, I'll be damned. Looks like we'll have our first date right here.

Chapter 9
Willow

"I CAN'T BELIEVE YOU DREAMT OF BECOMING A teacher. My parents are teachers. My mother taught third grade for many years, and my father recently retired from a long-tenured position at Clemson University. They had to drag the old man away. It makes me sad you've abandoned your dream." He lifts my hand and kisses the inside of my wrist, taunting me once again with sweet words and tiny glimpses of things that may or may not come to pass. I tap the balls of my feet on the sidewalk, pitter-pattering with cautious optimism and hopeful dreams that we'll end the night wet, naked, and utterly spent, but something tells me I wore this thong for nothing.

I nod and produce something that resembles a smile, grinding my teeth as the butterflies fluttering aimlessly in my tummy rally their forces. They're exhausted from six hours of flowers, wine, dinner, dancing, hugs, sweet nothings, and sexual chemistry that could charge the Vegas strip until Christmas.

Yet, something's missing. I know he shares my feelings. He's tender. Loving. He's a storybook hero in a three-piece

41

suit and sleeve tattoo peeking out from the cuff of his neatly pressed dress shirt. That sight alone soaked my panties and left me squirming in my seat, but I've detected no sexual neediness from him.

Clearly, I'm not as attractive as I've been led to believe. I could kill Nana for inflating my ego with those junior miss pageants. Do I stink? When did I become so easy to resist? Yesterday, he couldn't keep his hands off me---at least for those few minutes in the elevator. Did our act of shameless-ness bring about a long night of regret, and is this magical night nothing more than an elaborate kiss-off date meant to leave me with fond memories of our time together?

No. I won't allow it. I call dibs on this man. Lawson Kent is mine. Maybe it's too soon to make such declarations, but we don't decide when we fall in love. He called this fate, and I'm inclined to agree. He stole my heart like a thief in the night, and I feel rudderless without him. This gnawing ache is so much more than my filthy girl urges. It's cosmic and beautiful. It's the spiritual joining of two souls who need to become one before the female soul takes leave of her senses and does something she'll regret.

"Darling? Where did you go?" Lawson brings me close, nuzzling his barrel chest against the stiff peaks of my long-suffering breasts, desperate for the touch of those catcher-mitt hands, and I lose my ever-loving mind.

I rake my hand down the sleeves of his coat and claw into the tweed fabric of his suit. My forehead falls flat against his chest as a strange battle of emotions wages within me. I can't go along with his game one minute more. I need dick---his dick.

And I need it inside me.

"Law...take me..." My voice breaks. He's utterly clueless, and the thought of begging for sex yet again drowns me in unspeakable shame. I cut my words and change courses mid-sentence. "Take me back to the hotel, please. I've had enough."

"I thought we were having a lovely day." His lips land on the top of my head, and I feel him inhale the scent of my hair. He takes an unsteady breath, then gently exhales, lingering as he waits for me to speak.

I nod but hesitate to answer. I'll only say something crass or, worse, regrettable. Words of love clog my clenched throat, building strength like bubbles in an uncorked bottle of champagne that's seconds from bursting. It feels ridiculous. If I heard the words in my head from one of my girlfriends, I'd slap them upside the head and tell them to get a grip, but I know my heart. Better yet, I know my head. I know what's true, and I've never felt the burning desire to speak those three little words to a man. The mere idea mortified me to tears.

But not now. This feels right. Lawson Kent feels right.

"Sweetheart..." His lips graze my forehead as he gently rasps, repeating the word as his chest heaves against me. His thick fingers thread through the errant strands of hair that partially cover my face as he sweetly caresses my cheek, lifting my chin and gaze to meet his. "I could dance around this for weeks or months for the sake of propriety, but I know I'd come to the same conclusion. When you know, you know. And I know I've fallen in love with you. Do you think I'm a fool?"

"Lawson..." I grip his lapels and draw to the tips of my toes, wanting to climb him like a mighty oak. Because that's what he feels like. I hardly know him, but ever since we met, he's felt like the safe harbor I craved in the shitstorm that is my life. "If you're a fool, then I'm a fool."

"What does that mean?" Lawson snakes his arms tightly

around my waist and binds me tightly to him. The air leaves my lungs, and I lock my hands around his neck, bringing his lips inches from mine. Our eyes meet, and we each draw a deep breath before my lips part, and I say the words I've repeated in my mind all evening. "I love you. It's weird and wonderful, but I love you."

His eyes grow wide, wider than I've yet to see, and without a word, he lunges forward and crashes full force into me. Our mouths meet in a reckless collision of tongues and groans. He lifts my face, holding me in place as he assaults my lips, punishing them with blistering hot kisses that turn my simmering lust into a raging vat of molten steel. There's no denying me now. He needs me as much as I need him. We love each other. I've waited my whole life to truly make love and tonight's the night.

I break away and shift my gaze from side to side, smiling at a few passing tourists who stopped to ogle our vulgar display of affection, then dig my face into Lawson's jacket. "Should we go back to the hotel?" I know I said I didn't want to ask for sex again, but it seems far less loathsome now that we've declared our love and the probability of being refused feels highly unlikely.

He clasps my hand and leads me to the hired car. Towing me through the crowded sidewalk, he walks like a man with a mission, weaving in and out of sightseeing pedestrians towards the black limousine and fancy chauffeur idling by the curb. Tingles of exhilaration course through me, and happy tears sting my eyes. This is happening. We're running off to the hotel. My man is claiming me like a caveman and having his wretched way with me.

Oh my God, I hope it's wretched and dirty. So, so dirty.

When we reach the end of the sidewalk, Lawson waves to the driver to start the car and helps me into the backseat.

I nearly stumble in, eager to have a few moments alone before we reach the lobby, and overjoyed he's finally given in.

I shimmy across the leather bench seat, and Lawson slides in behind me. A stern expression clouds his features. He takes my hand and cradles it lovingly before he kicks sand in my face. "Darling, please don't be angry. We're going back, but I still think we should wait."

Fury replaces lust as my tea kettle of sexual urges begins to whistle. My bottom lip quivers, and my heart pounds with a mix of outrage and grief. What if he's gay? Am I a beard? I love him, but I can't spend my life with a gay man. And I refuse to apologize for my love of dick. If he's gay, he'll understand. "No, Lawson. I'm putting my foot down." I slam my pump on the floor mat and defiantly cross my arms over my chest. "If you don't find me sexually attractive, then just say it. But stop leading me on."

Throwing salt on the wound, his mouth tips into a smirk, and he wrestles me into his lap. "What foot? This little foot right here?" He yanks off my right pump and tickles my toes. "Is this the foot you're putting down?"

I chew my lip, stifling a giggle and wiggling my behind against the sizable erection that has yet to subside. It feels silly to ask, but I have to hear it from the horse's mouth. "Stop making jokes. Are you not into women? Because it's okay if you're not. I just can't be with a man who doesn't find me sexually attractive."

"For heaven's sake, Willow." He clutches the sides of my hips and digs my ass into his turgid cock. "I'm fucking dying. I've leaked so much cum into my boxers I'm fairly certain these trousers are ruined. Are you seriously asking me if I'm gay?"

I shrug, embarrassed I've placed him on the spot but still

expecting an answer. "Then why? Why don't you want to use it?"

He huffs an exasperated breath and leans his forehead to my cheek. "We've known each other two days. What's the rush, sweetheart?"

"That's nonsense. We've exchanged I love yous. That typically comes after the mattress mambo, and you know it!" My voice jumps an octave, and I whip my head to face the window, fearing he'll mistake my angry tears for something far more pathetic.

"Sugar?" He twists my body and nudges my chin to face him. "Let me explain."

"Don't sugar me." I yank the pocket square from his jacket and wipe my nose. "What gives? Why are you holding out? Are you trying to manipulate me?"

"Sweetheart, I know without a doubt that you are the girl for me." He holds his hand up like a boy scout taking an oath. "Our dear friend tried to fix us up for months, and when we said no, fate said yes. We're no accident or lucky coincidence. We're soul mates."

"Soul mates?"

"Tomorrow, we'll be home, and we have time to plan something nice. Let's do this right. Marry me next month, and we'll have the hottest honeymoon you can imagine. We'll make sweet passionate love, then I'll fuck you blind in every position, wherever you want, however you want, and for as long as you want, because you'll be entirely mine, and I'll be completely yours. And then I'll do it again the day after that and the day after that for eternity. I love you, Willow. But I think we should wait until we marry. For the sake of our future, I want to do this right."

My bottom lip trembles. I love this man, and he loves me. I should drown in happy tears and swoon into his arms.

Everything he confessed is so over the top romantic I'm sure my left ovary just exploded. *But I can't.* As I stare into the distance, my racing heart plummets with despair. My quivering core clenches, desperate for friction, desperate for him, and with no hope for relief.

"Baby?" He jostles me back to reality

"Marry me now." My words tumble loose without a second thought, and once they're free, I can't rein them in. I hardly recognize my voice, but it's no bluff. I want to be his wife.

Lawson looks me in the eye, drops the privacy screen, and calls to the driver, "Please take us to Tiffany's. I need to buy a ring."

Chapter 10
Lawson

Did I expect this? I'm not sure. I promise my intentions were almost entirely pure. Women have incredible willpower when it comes to sex. My Willow appears to be a charming anomaly, and I look forward to exploring this exception now that we're husband and wife.

Did I want her to hold out? Not really. I knew she'd break me, and I secretly prayed she would. If I possess any powers in mind control or talent for subtle suggestion, I'm wholeheartedly responsible. And I'll gladly bear the brunt because all this resulted in the culmination of my wildest dreams. Willow is mine.

"Get your ass over here, Mrs. Kent." I lift her into my arms and carry her into the suite. Her bright blue eyes sparkle as she tosses her tiny bouquet over her head and snakes her loving arms firmly around my neck. "You have no idea the fire you've kindled over the last two days, but you are about to find out." I swing her over my hips and slide my hands beneath her short dress, filling both hands with the round curves of her luscious ass. The touch of her naked skin brings a smile to my face, and I knead her supple flesh, hungry to lick every inch of it.

"Bring it on, Mr. Kent." Willow locks her ankles behind my back and brings her hands to my jaw. Our eyes meet in a dark heated gaze, and her pouty lips part. "I want this, Lawson. I'm not a virgin, but I haven't been with a man in years. If I appear a little inexperienced, I'm just out of practice..."

I cut her off and slam her roughly to my chest. With a stern look on my face, I walk us to the bed and drop her onto the mattress.

"Darling, as far as you and I are concerned, we're both virgins. No one else mattered. No one came before us. This is the first time we're making love, and if I can help it, we'll never be with anyone else again. No sharing. No open marriages. No cheating. You're mine, and I will always be yours." I furiously unwind my tie, then yank it off in one swipe.

She scrambles to her knees and pulls her dress over her head. Working with purpose, she balls it in her fist and tosses it across the room. "I'm yours, Lawson. I'm ready." She hops towards me, and her busy fingers tear through the buttons on my shirt. Her eyes grow wide with glassy-eyed wonder when she pulls the sleeves off my arms and gets her first glimpse of the ink painted up and down my arms. She surveys thoughtfully, and my heart beats like a jackrabbit until she finally speaks.

"I didn't think I could get any wetter, Mr. Kent." She ducks her head and flutters her lashes.

I spy the damp spot between her thighs, the only mate-rial holding that thong together, and crawl onto the mattress. "I guarantee you're about to get so much wetter than this." I reach into her panties and run my finger through her wet slit, oozing cum from my cock when my girl shudders in my arms. The scent of her arousal hits me, and a rush of adrenaline awakens my primal urge to mate. A growl from the pit of my stomach breaks free, "You won't be needing these." I rip the flimsy fabric off her legs and hike her thigh over my shoulder. The sight is nothing less than perfection. Willow's pink pussy is nearly bare, slighted parted, dripping wet with a tiny thatch of flaxen curls. My cock twitches like a bucking bronco, and I almost come in my pants.

I'm in awe of my good fortune.

"Law, I love you," she breathes the words and twists into the sheet, trying in vain to shield her half-naked body from my lecherous view. The flush in her skin travels from her chest onto her face, tainting her cheeks bright red as she drops her bright eyes and gives me her undivided attention. I'm the luckiest bastard in the world. As unworthy as I am, I made this beautiful woman fall in love with me.

"I love you, baby." I scrape my teeth against the sensitive skin of her inner thigh, and she wiggles into my waiting hands. "I hope you like it dirty."

"Fuck yes, make it dirty," her soft cry becomes a frantic wail when I spread her thighs and take one long lick down the seam of her sex. Her arousal coats my tongue and spills onto my beard. I might leave it there for days. I use my fingers to stroke her clit, flicking it in tiny strokes before replacing it with my tongue. I suckle. Lick. Fuck her with my mouth as she grinds her slippery pussy against my face, screaming for mercy then begging for more.

"Oh my God, yes! Lawson! No! Yes! Wait! Stop! Don't stop! I love you!" she whines and weaves her fingers through my hair, pulling in time with my devotion. With every lick, her praise grows louder, and my heart threatens to burst free from my chest.

"Is this married pussy hungry for cock?" I guide two fingers into her slick channel and pump into her clenching walls. She rides my hand, jolting off the mattress as my tongue continues to work her clit. I feel unhinged, desperate to plunge into her hot sex and spill two days of cum, but I can't tear my eyes away from her writhing body long enough to rip off my pants.

"Lawson, I'm hungry. Starving." She nods through pants as she wipes away the tears streaming down her cheeks. With what little strength she can muster, she unhooks her bra and flings it at my face. "Give me what's mine, Mr. Kent. Perform your husbandly duties."

I stand at the edge of the bed and unfasten my belt, smothering a grin while I examine the flawless beauty before me---her long legs, the sharp curve of her waist, her full breasts, and taut nipples waiting for my touch. My mouth waters with avarice and visions of all the filthy, forbidden things we'll do together over the next fifty years. "Is this what my girl wants?" I drop my pants, pull down my boxers, and hold my rigid cock in my hands.

"Law..." Willow pops into a sitting position. Her dazed expression sobers as she takes in the view. "That's for me?" She licks her lips, and my heart swells with pride.

I climb onto the bed and wedge myself between her thighs, seconds from unleashing a tide of lust that will carry us through dawn. I thread my fingers through hers and stretch her arms over her head, bringing my mouth inches from hers. "You better believe it's for you."

Chapter 11
Willow

"Lawson!" He hooks my knee over his arm and sinks into my pussy, stalling when his hefty slab of meat meets the snug confines of my tight walls. When he hesitates, I wiggle into him, wantonly lifting my hips in search of my prize. I know I saw so much more, and I won't be denied.

"You said you weren't..." his voice trembles with anxiety. "You wouldn't lie to me?" He seals his lips to mine, thrusting once, twice, rutting and teasing, for fear he'll break me. "I'll die if I hurt you."

"Baby..." I whimper with exasperation, then squeal when he plunges deep into my drenched sex. I ease my legs over his back, working him in, wiggling my ass to feel every centimeter of his turgid flesh stretching me open. As the discomfort passes, I'm left with a pain-tinged, euphoric-soaked friction that makes my eyes roll all the way back in my head.

Lawson's magnificence knows no equal. His powerful body moves like a well-oiled engine, pumping in and out, out and in, moving in time with our breaths and heartbeats while we clamor for one more kiss, one more lick---anything to feel connected and bound. His sweat falls across my breasts, my arousal soaks our thighs, and the squelching sounds of sex fill the room.

"So good, Law. I knew you'd feel good," I moan and claw the sheet for purchase as he brings my knees to my shoulders. He shows me no mercy, and I ask for none. I beg for more, harder, faster, and wilder. I want to wake up sore from hours of Lawson's naughty abuse.

"Your pussy feels like fucking magic. Tell me you're on the pill because there's no way I'm pulling out." His abdomen flexes with every brutal thrust, and a sudden chill makes my nipples tighten painfully. Children? It's a secret desire. Not even my closest friends know I want to be a mother. It doesn't mesh with cool Willow's image. But I don't want to be her anymore. She never truly existed.

I shake my head and rake my nails across his skin, letting my hand feel the movement of his heaving chest. "I am, but I'm horrible about taking it. Do your worst, Mr. Kent. I... I love you." Our eyes meet, and a second shudder passes through me. I feel like a virgin. For the first time, I'm making love to a man I love and respect---who feels those emotions in equal measure. Everything I've ever avoided has come to pass. Love. Commitment. Marriage. My heart feels like an open wound. And while dread consumes me, there's so much fulfillment in my vulnerability. So much more than I expected. His love fills all the empty spaces inside me. And I want to build a life with him.

"You're the one who's magic, doll." He settles his weight over me, twisting me onto his lap as we entwine our limbs and seal our bodies. Our hips keep moving, grinding furiously. He grips my waist and bounces me, slamming me up and down, sliding my slick pussy on his steely cock, and meeting me halfway. I fall forward and rest my palms on his chest, wriggling in circles, testing the boundaries of my sanity as sweat drips down my face. I'm so close. The tension feels like a lit rocket, pulsing deep within, ready for launch.

"Come for me, darling. I'm about to burst inside you. Come for me, Willow." Lawson holds my breasts, pinches my nipples, and thrusts. He thrusts so hard he tosses me onto his chest and rolls me onto the mattress. I scream as he hits that perfect spot, once, twice, three times, four--- it's too much. I sink my teeth into his shoulder and screech like an owl. My legs kick and spread wider, taking him in deeper, as my clenching pussy milks his cock dry.

"Law..." I smack my lips, panting, dripping with cum and sweat, utterly spent but desperate to say something meaningful.

"I love you, baby." He curls me into his arms and flips me over onto my knees. "I hope you're ready for more."

Chapter 12
Lawson
Nine Days Later

I STARE ONTO THE STREET FROM MY OFFICE WINDOW and watch the sidewalk fill with busy commuters, rushing to the local dives and diners to stuff their faces. New York has some of the best food in the world, and one should take time to enjoy their meal. A week ago, I wasn't any different. I didn't realize I'd been sleepwalking through life until I met Willow. Food tastes better, richer, bursting with flavor. The sky looks a brighter shade of blue, and the sun feels warmer on my face. She's a walking miracle come to life.

But something's wrong. I know I make her happy, but she doubts our marriage. She doubts our longevity and, worst of all, doubts our love. Everything happened too fast. It's impractical. Unreasonable and unwise.

"Why am I here?" Lincoln folds his long legs into a leather captain's chair in front of my desk and casually flips through the pages of his favorite magazine.

"What would you do?" I ask in earnest. He may only be forty-three, but he's wise beyond his years.

"Are you serious?" His stunned expression becomes a disapproving glare. "I had such a miserable divorce. It took me years to date, and the first one out of the gate turned out to be more insane than my ex-wife. Don't take advice from me. I don't know anything about women." He drops his gaze and returns to the article in his lap.

Why do I put so much faith in his opinion? I cross the room, swinging my arms in anger, and rip the magazine out from his hands. "Please, focus. I could lose my wife if I don't nip this in the bud."

He shrugs and leans into his seat. "You've known Willow a week, Lawson. You'll get over it."

A feminine gasp escapes before I can rein it in. My eyes narrow with contempt. My blood boils. I twist the magazine in my hands, toss it to the floor, and smash it under my foot. "You're a horse's ass. Willow was always meant to be my wife. If I'd only known her one day, I would have felt her loss for a lifetime."

He lifts his hands in mock surrender and sighs, "Fine, I apologize. Don't get your panties in a bunch. You said yourself, this all began when she visited her parents. They obviously made her feel foolish for marrying you so quickly. If she spent her whole life trying to get her parents' love and approval and her marriage to you disappointed them, it's bound to make her second-guess everything. You're talking about years of psychological conditioning. One week and your great love doesn't erase her knee-jerk reactions."

"But I asked her what they said, and she swore they were happy for us." I pace left to right, replaying the evening in my mind, and try to remember the look in her eyes when she broke down their conversation. "Why would she lie?"

"Because she didn't want to hurt your feelings. Because she didn't give their criticism any weight. But those digs fester longer than we care to admit. What kind of lawyer are you? You know better than this." He lifts his wrist to check the time and taps his watch. "I thought you were taking me to lunch."

I drink the rest of my coffee and check my phone. No new messages from Willow. She sent me a text shortly after her first meeting, but nothing since. I get fewer every day. I know it's hard to keep up the enthusiasm, but we've been married nine days, not nine years. She hasn't even fully moved into my brownstone.

Is that why she's nervous? We already live together. It's not like she owns her apartment. Perhaps she feels vulnerable. I should draw up some papers giving her my place in case of a divorce---heaven forbid. I don't even want to consider that scenario. Willow and I are for life. I know it in my heart and feel it in my soul.

Little darling, what on earth is going on in your mind?

Snapping fingers bring me back. "I'm hungry, dickhead, and I've got a client at 2:30." Lincoln lifts his magazine off the floor and tries his best to unwrinkle the pages.

"Fine, we'll go downtown." I grab my coat and head for the door. Willow's having lunch with her girlfriends near Wall Street today. Our mutual friend, Macy, let it slip when I called her earlier. Well, she let it slip after I prodded, begged, and manipulated her with fake tears. It doesn't matter. The point is I know where she'll be, and it gives me the perfect excuse to pop in and say hello. The last thing I want to do is act like a nuisance. I'll sit on the other side of the room with my brother and give her privacy. I only want to make sure she knows I'm thinking of her.

That feels as pathetic as it sounds in my mind.

"Downtown? I work uptown!" Lincoln stomps behind me, groaning as he slams my office door.

"Pipe down."

"Why the hell don't you call her grandparents and invite them to dinner? She was raised by them, wasn't she? Win them over. I've heard rumors you can be quite charming. If they love her, they'll see she's happy and give her the blessing she craves." He dawdles behind me, smoothing the pages of his ridiculous magazine against his pants.

I spin around and hug him so tightly I lift him off the ground. "Thank you, Linc. This is why you're my favorite brother. Don't tell Lionel."

Chapter 13
Willow

I STARE AT MY SCREEN AND TOUCH EACH LETTER FROM Lawson's last text. I love you. He's so certain. No doubts or reservations. He's never wavered since we returned from Nevada---not once.

He deserves so much better than me.

I raise my hand to my chest and rub my palm against my sternum, massaging the place where my heart used to be. The space feels empty, like a cavernous hole that echoes every time I cry.

We were so happy. No, we are happy. Why am I ruining things? Why would I sabotage the best thing that's ever happened to me with self-doubt and emotional baggage I've longed to dump for years?

Lawson hasn't changed. If anything, he's more wonderful than I ever imagined. But the longer we're together, the harder it will be to let him go when this whole thing falls apart. And it has to fall apart. Nothing this wonderful lasts forever, especially with such an impractical beginning. Everyone says my parents loved each other once too. They loved each other so much they put me second.

And now they hardly speak to one another. Although they found the time to unite when they found out I was married. They shared one voice about the eventual failure of my ridiculous marriage.

Hardly anyone has anything good to say.

Baron laughed at my announcement. No, if I remember correctly, he guffawed and equated it to something out of a cheesy B-movie. When he wouldn't stop teasing me, Seth pounced and revealed Baron's deep dark secret to the entire room. He's madly in love with Sunny Luna. Sunny is Seth and Sebastian's nineteen-year-old sister. She recently moved from L.A. to New York, which coincides with Baron's alcohol-fueled pity parties. That's a shocker, to say the least. But no one was more shocked than Sebastian, who quit on the spot and warned him to stay away from his baby sister.

The girls at work smiled awkwardly and wished me well, then took bets behind my back on how long it would last. I hear my assistant gave us a year. That's sweet of her--- I guess.

I don't have the heart to tell my grandparents. I'm dying to introduce them to Lawson, and he'd probably win them over in seconds, but what if he doesn't? What if they react no differently than my parents? I don't think I could bear it if they didn't support my marriage. They both mean the world to me.

Sometimes I feel the only one who's rooting for us is Macy.

"Mrs. Kent!" Macy swoops in for a hug, throwing her arms and bags around my neck as she jumps for joy. This isn't the first time we've seen each other since my return, but her enthusiasm is just the same. "You're glowing! Positively glowing!" She threads her arm into mine and leads us into the tiny French bistro we frequent near the Exchange. Jana is already here, warming the high-top table and looking down from her perch with a glare of condescension. She's said all the right things, but I can tell by her tone she thinks I'm a fool.

"I am not glowing. I'm stressed," I sigh and deposit my purse and coat onto an empty chair.

"How are you doing? Have you spoken to your grand-parents yet?" Jana sips her coffee and peruses the menu, failing to lift her gaze to address me properly.

"Will you stop being weird with me? I got married. I fell in love with a wonderful man, and we were so overcome with emotion we ran to the nearest altar. I know that doesn't sound like the person you know, but that's what happened. That doesn't mean I want out. I just need to adjust. You decided to marry Vlad and Ilya and Maxim within days of hooking up, so you should know all about the power of love at first sight." I settle into my chair and cross my legs, fidgeting with my clothes as I try to brush away the heap of anxious energy sitting on my shoulders.

"Sorry, you know I love you, and I'm over the moon if you're happy, but it just seems out of character. And it wasn't love at first sight. I'd known Ilya and Max--" Jana tries to correct me, but Macy quickly cuts her off.

"No, no, ma'am. You did not know Vlad. Don't forget I was there. I helped you get ready for your meeting. And he's the one you're marrying first!" Macy jumps in for the rescue. "Besides, get off your high horse or your thoroughbred Arabian stallion, Miss soon-to-be Queen of Manhattan. I know I said I'd stop judging you when I became engaged to Hunter. Marrying a man more than twice my age is scandalous. But for the sake of Willow's peace of mind, I'll have to return to my earlier assessment. Marrying three men is far more outrageous than marrying a man after two dates in Las Vegas."

"Yeah!" I chime in, nodding furiously.

"I'm not judging," Jana lies and tries to backtrack.

"Yes, you are! And I didn't judge you." I quietly think back to our earlier conversations and clear my conscience. I judged Macy, not her. I shrink in my seat and make a mental note to send her something nice.

"Besides, this is Lawson Kent. He's a sweetheart. A gentleman. Smart as a whip and funny as shit. I hate not working in the same building with him anymore. No one gets my true crime references at Hunter's office. You know damn well if you hadn't met the boys, you would've chased Lawson, big time. If I hadn't given my heart to Hunter years ago, I would have ridden the Lawson train all the way to South Carolina to meet his mama."

Macy turns to me and squeezes my hand. "Please tell me he's good in the sack. He's such a grizzly bear. I picture him going fucking crazy in bed." Her eyes grow wide with wonder, and Jana leans in, ears perked to hear details.

I scoot back into my chair and clutch the pearls Lawson bought me as a wedding gift. "Back off skanks, you're talking about my husband. I'm not divulging details about his impressive equipment or superhuman stamina. That shit's private." I smile to myself and reach into my purse, scrambling to find my phone. My text average has sharply declined lately, and I have a hunch Lawson has noticed.

I tap on the screen and spot a missed call from my grandmother. It's time to tell my grandparents. I'll call them after lunch and make plans for the weekend. If they love me, they'll love Lawson. Because I really do love him.

Angry with myself for letting my parents' bullshit seep into my heart, I pull up his message and answer.

I love you, Mr. Kent. Miss you.

Then look behind you.

"Lawson!" Macy jumps out of her chair and sprints towards the door. "Oh my God, I've missed you so much. Didn't I tell you I had a girl for you?"

He dips down to give her a hug, chuckling as he answers, "You did. You know I'm a stubborn old goat. But as always, you were right."

"Excuse me. He's mine." I wedge myself between them and wrap my arms around his chest.

"Hello, darling. How's my girl?" He kisses the top of my head and rocks me back and forth like a child. As always, he curls me into his embrace and hugs me tight enough to mend my wounded heart.

"Better with you here. I'm sorry I've been weird. Until you came along. I didn't believe in love," I whisper and greedily sink into his warmth.

His soft brown gaze, the one that first reeled me in, spears my heart again. "Everything's fine, darling. Just believe in me. Just believe in us." I place my head on his chest, and the familiar beat of his heart radiates into mine. Everyone's negative words flitter away like ash in the wind.

I don't care what anyone says. I'll love this man until I die.

"FOR HEAVEN'S SAKE, I THINK MY NANA WAS FLIRTING with you." Willow slips off her shoes and unties the sash on her dress. "Grandpa practically had to haul her away kicking and screaming when she offered you that third slice of pie. You'd think she never met a man with a southern accent before. The woman was shameless." She giggles as she unfastens her earrings and drops them into her jewelry box.

"Your Nana is a sweet-natured woman, darling. She was only being kind for your sake. It was a lovely evening." We pass each other on the way to the closet, jabbering while we undress. But my eyes never leave the sweet sway of her hips or the way her dress lingers over the sharp curve of her ass before it slides to the floor. Like clockwork, the blood in my brain rushes south. My mind grows hazy, and my cock stiffens at record speed. I stumble closer, following the familiar trail of her perfume, and hear her voice.

"Sweetheart, where did I leave the new negligee you bought me? I wanted to wear it tonight. It feels like a special night." Willow calls from inside the closet, and I catch sight of her naked breasts, bouncing freely as she searches for the box I can't for the life of me remember where I placed.

I watch her search and quietly remove the rest of my clothes. Even in a state of manufactured panic, she takes my breath away. "You look perfect just like that." I step out of my boxers and hold the lead pipe, weighing me down. No one has ever turned me on like Willow. And there's something about being married---knowing she's mine, and I'm hers---that makes everything a thousand times hotter.

"Who are you today? Am I being visited by sweet Lawson or bad Lawson?" She releases the ribbon in her hair, and flaxen waves fall on her shoulders. Her soft blue eyes gleam under her fluttering lashes as she saunters towards me. Never in my wildest dreams did I imagine such a happy coincidence would become something so wonderful.

"Do you have to ask?" I step closer and place my hand between her thighs. Arousal drips on my fingers, soaking my hand, as I trace the seam of her sex, back and forth, nudging her hard clit with each pass.

"Such a bad girl. How long have you been wet?" I finger her, holding her steady on wobbly legs.

She nods, grasping my shoulders and climbing my hips as she cries, "Since the drive home. You looked so good in your suit, baby. I couldn't help it." Willow wastes no time. She winds her legs around my waist and slides her soaked pussy down my cock. I grunt, surprised by how deep she takes me and stunned by her grip. Her wide eyes meet mine, and her pussy ripples, clenching as she sucks me in over and over.

"You really wanted cock, didn't you?" I wince as I watch her bounce recklessly, believing I would be the aggressor instead of the man being used as an amusement ride. I try to breathe, panting through groans and dirty talk. I shouldn't have had so much pie.

"I did. I craved your cock all day." She screams, scratching my shoulders and shuddering wildly as her pussy tenses around my shaft.

"I think about this pussy all day, every day. Nothing will ever change that." I slam into her, burying myself as far as I'll go and shoot streams of hot cum into my gorgeous wife. She looks so fucking beautiful. I almost come again.

"Lawson!" Willow trembles in my arms, whimpering against our kiss as we lose ourselves in a space where only we live. It's my favorite place in the whole damn world.

Locked in each other's arms and sealed in a kiss, we fall onto the floor, limbs entangled, souls entwined, and make love again.

Hell yes, this was fate.

Chapter 15
Epilogue- Five Years Later
Willow

"MAY WE COME IN?" LAWSON'S SMILE APPEARS AT THE door. Flanked by our twins, Lauren and Lucy, he produces a fall bouquet and tiptoes into my classroom. It's my first week teaching kindergarten, and he knew I planned to stay late to catch up on work. He made me promise not to stay too long, and this is his way of making sure.

"What a sweet surprise." My girls rush to both sides of my desk and give me a hug, anxious to see me after our long day apart. I waited until they were four and enrolled in our pre-school program to start my new job, but our separation hasn't been easy. "Did you have a good day?"

They nod in unison then squeal with disgust when Lawson leans in to give me a kiss on the lips. Mommy and Daddy always do the ickiest things. We smirk and kiss again, torturing our daughters with our open affection. Their innocent little minds have no idea how icky we can be.

"How's my girl? Are you enjoying yourself?" Lawson offers his hand and pulls me into his arms. "I'm so freaking proud of you, darling."

"It's hard, but I kind of love it." I smile and rest my head against his chest. I may be tired from herding five-year-olds, but it's so much more gratifying than corralling unruly celebrities who need to grow the hell up.

I couldn't have done this without Lawson's support. He's a one-man cheer section. He helped me study, drove me to classes while I was pregnant, listened to podcasts in the car to make sure I was safe, and helped prepare me for interviews. And when things got particularly stressful, we even did a little role play to blow off steam.

I don't know how I got so lucky.

"Are you ready to go? The girls really want to pick out pumpkins for the stoop, and I promised we'd go to that place down the block before it gets dark." Lawson nervously claps his hands and pretends we didn't discuss waiting until next week for pumpkin picking.

I grab my coat from the closet and hand it to Lawson. While he holds it open, I slide my arms in and stare narrow-eyed at my conniving daughters. "Who did it? Who talked your father into getting the pumpkin early?"

They freeze and point to each other.

Lawson attempts to intervene on their behalf. "I caved. It's my fault."

I caress his face, stroking his beard lovingly while my evil spawns look on. "You're their pawn, sweetheart. You think you're in charge, but they know how to manipulate you. They've been doing this since they were two. They have too much of me in them." I shake my head and sigh. "We agreed last night we'd wait until next week, or the pumpkin would rot in this humidity. The only reason they want it now is because their little friend across the street said she's getting hers tomorrow."

Lauren and Lucy look at one another then look at their

father, unsure of what to say. "Can we get ice cream instead?"

"Of course, sweethearts. Let's get some ice cream. That's only fair." He rounds them up and leads the four of us out of my class.

"For heaven's sake, Law. It's fifty degrees outside." I shudder to think what they'll be like as teenagers.

On our way home, watching our girls lick their cones, shivering but thrilled, Lawson takes my hand and threads our fingers tight. "It's almost our fifth anniversary."

I lean into his shoulder and hum, "I know. Are you still taking me to see fake Frank Sinatra?"

"I am, indeed. I've booked us into the same suite, and fake Frank will be there. Is there anything else you want to do? The Grand Canyon? Hoover Dam? We can even extend it to Lake Tahoe or Sedona." He draws me in for a kiss.

"Yes, make sure you pack Bad Lawson. I haven't seen him in a while." I angle my face to give him a wink and nudge him with my elbow. Unfortunately, our daughters make it almost impossible for things to get too crazy in bed, and I look forward to those moments when I can scream at the top of my lungs. Bad Lawson always makes that part easy.

He lifts our locked hands and kisses my fingers. "Darling, he's missed you something fierce."

THANKS FOR READING!

Would you like to read Macy's story?
    Read about Macy and her older man, Hunter
    in Dad Bod Billionaire
    Now Available

You can catch up with Jana and the loves of her life in
Room Four: Playing with the Big Boys
Now Available
You can read all about Enzo and Gala's steamy love affair in
Vanished in Manhattan,
Available February 24, 2022
AND Lawson's big brother Lincoln gets his own Happily Ever
in We'll Always Have Paris
Coming May 1

After I Do Series

*This coming February, you're officially invited to attend a month-long celebration of love! Twenty-eight of your favorite short, steamy romance authors have teamed up to bring you stories that will make you swoon, laugh, and set your e-readers on fire! Whether they've stumbled into love, fallen for their worst enemy, corralled their bestie or are fighting to rekindle a lost love... Tag along and find out what happens **"After I Do."***

Check out the Entire After I Do Series here

The "I Do" Do-Over by Poppy Parks

First Blush by Reina Torres

Return of the Mobster by Imani Jay

Marriage Pact by Piper Cook

Wedding Belle by Violet Rae

The Shadow of Us by Tamrin Banks

Wedded Miss by Karla Doyle

When We Woke Up by Ember Davis

All I Need is You by Pippa Lux

Happenstance by Matilda Martel

Keeping What's Mine by Carly Keene

There's More For Us by Allie York

Cracks in the Windshield by Bree Weeks

Mediocre by Bree Weeks

Winning My Wife by Layne Daniels

The Unforeseen Arrangement by Jade Royal

Just For You by Haven Rose

Worth the Wait by Silke Champion

Have You Met My Wife? by MK Moore

More Than Love Ja'Nese Dixon

Love is All We Got by Kindra White

Wearing the King's Ring by Gia Bailey

Pre-Arranged Love by Andrea Marie

No Ordinary Love Story by Kelsey Calloway

Run Away With Me by Macy Fox

The Biker Takes A Bride by Jail West

To Tempt A Husband by Lindsay Evans

Also by Matilda Martel

DO YOU LOVE STEAMY AGE GAP ROMANCE?

Those are my favorites.

If you like them as much as me,

you might like these titles:

My Second Chance

Takeover

Blindsided

We'll Always Have Paris

Dad Bod Billionaire

Get Your Kicks

The Pastor

In Praise of Older Men

My Heart's Desire

The Senator

Maestro

Gilded Cage

Love Match

Play Right

The Man I Love

Bad Boss

Clever Girl

Chasing Zoe

The Good Girl

My Ward

Do you love Billionaire Romances?

Try these titles:

Takeover

Off the Market

Filthy Rich

Filthy Love

Blindsided

Gilded Cage

Magic Man

Hostile Takeover

There She Goes

Agreeably Arranged

Bad Boy

And don't miss out on my latest release, an over the top steamy Billionaire Reverse Harem:

Room Four: Playing with the Big Boys

Do you love Friends to Lovers?

Shut Up & Kiss Me

Unsuitable

Lucky Man

Marry Me

Baby Steps

Off the Market

Do you love Mafia Romances?

Check out my BROOKLYN BAD BOYS

Love Interrupted

Love Unleashed

Love Revealed

Vanished in Manhattan

Secret Weapon

BAD BOYS TURNED GOOD?

Check out SCOUNDRELS IN LOVE

Bad Professor

Bad Boss

Bad Boy

PHILLY BOYS FIND LOVE IN LOVE BITES

Love Hate

Love Nest

Love Match

And many more - find them HERE

Thanks for reading and I hope you come back again!

About the Author

Matilda is a Texas girl in love with a Philly boy who loves to write dirty books about two people who trip into love and fumble their way into a Filthy, Funny, Happily Ever After.

I live in Austin, with my husband, two crazy Chihuahuas and an even crazier cat. And I spend most of my day writing dirty romance books about older men who fall in love with younger women and make fools of themselves trying to win their hearts.

If you love Dark Romance, you've come to the wrong place. I don't like dark heroes.

I like my hero to be successful, sweet, suave, sophisticated and kind--- and then I want him to lose all his composure and game when he meets the heroine. I want him to turn into a bumbling idiot when he spots the girl of his dreams and revert to a teenage boy in a man's body trying to win her.

I like my heroines to be witty, intelligent, and unshakeable---who could do just as well without a man—until the hero convinces her otherwise.

I write A LOT OF AGE GAP--because I LOVE AGE GAP ROMANCE. I've got no other excuse for it.

No matter what kind of story it is, my ladies are ADORED, and my endings are always Happily EVER AFTER, not HFN.

To receive a free ebook, join Matilda Martel's newsletter.

Please head to my website to learn what's in the final stages and will be coming out soon!